susanna gretz · alison sage

teddy bears
cure a cold

FOUR WINDS PRESS · NEW YORK

"I feel sick," said William.
"You can't be sick," said Andrew;
"we're going to try out our new tools."

"But I *am* sick,"
said William,
"and I am going to bed."

William did not eat his breakfast.

"Maybe he really is sick," said Robert.
"Don't believe it," said Louise;
"he just wants breakfast in bed."
"Let's go see," said Charles.

"You don't look so sick to me," said Louise.
"My throat hurts," William complained.

That afternoon, William was still in bed.
"Let's play monkey in the middle,"
said Andrew. "It will cheer you up."
"My head hurts," said William.

The next morning, Charles made William
a special breakfast.
"I'm not hungry," said William.
"William is always hungry,"
whispered Louise.
"He *must* be sick."

Charles found a thermometer.
Louise took out her flashlight.
"William, you have white spots
on your throat," she said.
"And he has a temperature, too," said Charles.
"We'll have to take good care of him."

Louise and John made the bed.
Robert found a hot-water bottle.
"I'll be in charge of the temperature
chart," said Charles.
Andrew made a honey-and-lemon drink.
"Thank you," croaked William.

That evening,
William felt worse.
One minute
he was hot;
the next minute
he was cold.
His sheets were sticky
and talking gave him
a headache.
The other bears tiptoed
away, and William
finally fell asleep.

The picture frame on the wall reads:

GREAT-UNCLE
JEROME

Tap-tap. Tap-tap-tap.
What was that?
William sat upright in bed.
"GO AWAY!" he shouted.

The light went on.
"I heard something tapping," said William.
"It must have been the wind," said Robert.
"And I *saw* things," said William.
"It's because you're sick," said Charles.

The next day,
there was a chocolate pig for William,
and Sara brought him some flowers.
"I hope you like tulips," she said.
Charles gave him a bell.
"Ring if you need anything," he said.
"Thank you," said William;
and for the next few days
he stayed in bed.

Then one morning, Sara made him some oatmeal.
"Thank you," said William.
"But could you make me a banana milkshake?"

Robert brought him
some apples.
"Thank you,"
said William;
"but will you
peel one for me?"

Andrew brought him some cards.
"Thank you," said William.
"But I'd rather have a new jigsaw puzzle . . .
  and a bag of peanuts."
"Hmm," said Louise.

ting-ting

ting-a-ling

ding

dang

dong

jingle

jangle

DING

di

DIN

That afternoon, William rang his bell.
"Sara," he called. "Could you bring me a blanket?"
He rang his bell again.
"Charles! Robert! Can you open the
window? It's too hot now.
John! Will you read me a story?"

DIIIING

DING

DONG

DANG

DONG DANG

DANG

GRISLY

JIGSAW

William rang his bell again.
"What does he want *now*?" said Andrew.
"He wants potato chips," said Louise.
"Who's going to get them?" said Sara;
"it's cold outside and –
look! It's snowing."

"They're very quiet downstairs,"
thought William.
"Where's my lunch?"
He looked out of
the window.

There they were!
Out in the snow.

William waited and waited.
At last Louise came in with a tray.
"Where are my potato chips?" said William.
"Sorry," said Louise,
"but we made rice pudding instead.
It will be better for your throat."

Andrew peeked into the room.
"Come on, Louise. We're ready."
"Ready for *what*?" said William.
"We'll tell you later," said Louise.

William looked at the rice pudding.
Then he looked at his puzzle;
the pieces were all over the bed
and there were crumbs *everywhere*.
"Where *is* everyone?"

CRASH! clatter clatter THUMP.

"What's that?"
He heard the sound of sawing.

screeee-scrawww screeeee-scrawww

"They're making something!"
said William.

Was it a shelf?
A letterbox? A birdhouse?
. . . a giant birdhouse?

. . . a trampoline?
William jumped out of bed and ran downstairs.

"William! what are you doing out of bed?
  Have you seen what we've made?"
  William's mouth was too full to answer.
"Come and see," said Sara.

It was a sled!

"Who's going to steer first?"
  said Louise.
"I am," said William.
"But you're sick," said Louise.
"I *was* sick," said William.
"I'm feeling much better now, thank you."

All afternoon they went sledding.

When they got home, William said,
"Tea time."
Everyone was hungry except Louise.
"But there's doughnuts and chocolate
cake," said William.
"I don't want any," said Louise.
"I'm going to bed.
I think I'm sick."